B
Backyard
Animals

Jane Katirgis

Bailey Books
an imprint of
Enslow Publishers, Inc.
40 Industrial Road
Box 398
Berkeley Heights, NJ 07922
USA

http://www.enslow.com

Bailey Books, an imprint of Enslow Publishers, Inc.

Copyright © 2011 by Enslow Publishers, Inc.

Library of Congress Cataloging-in-Publication Data

Katirgis, Jane.
  Baby backyard animals / by Jane Katirgis.
      p. cm. — (All about baby animals)
  Includes bibliographical references and index.
  Summary: "Introduces simple concepts about backyard animals using short sentences and repetition of words"—Provided by publisher.
  ISBN 978-0-7660-3795-3
  1. Urban animals—Infancy—Juvenile literature. 2. Garden animals—Infancy—Juvenile literature. I. Title.
  QL49.K325 2011
  591.3'9—dc22
                                    2010016254
Paperback ISBN: 978-1-59845-158-0

Printed in the United States of America

052010 Lake Book Manufacturing, Inc., Melrose Park, IL

10 9 8 7 6 5 4 3 2 1

To Our Readers: We have done our best to make sure all Internet Addresses in this book were active and appropriate when we went to press. However, the author and the publisher have no control over and assume no liability for the material available on those Internet sites or on other Web sites they may link to. Any comments or suggestions can be sent by e-mail to comments@enslow.com or to the address on the back cover.

❂ Enslow Publishers, Inc., is committed to printing our books on recycled paper. The paper in every book contains 10% to 30% post-consumer waste (PCW). The cover board on the outside of each book contains 100% PCW. Our goal is to do our part to help young people and the environment too!

Photo Credits: iStockphoto.com: © Andy Gehrig, p. 10, © Kenneth C. Zirkel, p. 22, © Michael Zurawski, p. 12; Shutterstock, pp. 1, 3, 4, 6, 8, 14, 16, 18, 20.

Cover Photo: Shutterstock.com

Note to Parents and Teachers

Help pre-readers get a jumpstart on reading. These lively stories introduce simple concepts with repetition of words and short simple sentences. Photos and illustrations fill the pages with color and effectively enhance the text. Free Educator Guides are available for this series at www.enslow.com. Search for the *All About Baby Animals* series name.

Contents

Words to Know 3

Story 5

Read More 24

Web Sites 24

Index 24

Words to Know

grass

tree

What do you see in the grass?

I see baby rabbits.

I see a baby duck.

I see a baby fox.

I see a baby
ground squirrel.

I see a baby deer.

I see a baby bug.

I see a baby turtle.

Look up!

What do you see in the tree?

I see baby birds!

Read More

Glogas, Valerie. *In My Backyard.* Mount Pleasant, S.C.: Sylvan Dell, 2007.

Kalman, Bobbie, and Kelley MacAulay. *Backyard Habitats.* St. Catharines, ON.: Crabtree Publishing, 2007.

Web Sites

National Geographic. Animals.
<http://animals.nationalgeographic.com>
Click on "Animal Photos.

National Wildlife Federation. *Wildlife Watch.*
<http://www.nwf.org/wildlifewatch/>

Index

birds, 23

bugs, 17

deer, 15

ducks, 9

fox, 11

grass, 5

rabbits, 7

squirrel, 13

tree, 21

turtle, 19

Guided Reading Level: **B**
Guided Reading Leveling System is based on the guidelines recommended by Fountas and Pinnell.

Word Count: 53